The Coffee Shop Chronicles

For information, contact: Stan Lowery
(stanleylowery365@Gmail.com)

First Edition
Book and Cover design by Stan Lowery
ISBN: 979-8-9946092-0-0

The Coffee Shop Chronicles

Stanley D. Lowery

Table of Contents

THE COFFEE SHOP CHRONICLES

Table of Contents

At 3 am, I wake in a cold sweat, my heart racing, and I struggle to make sense of the jumbled images flashing through my mind. I sit up abruptly, the remnants of the haunting dream still lingering in the air around me, elusive and disorienting. It is the same recurring dream that has been plaguing me for weeks, a puzzle without a solution.

I find myself sitting on the edge of the bed, my head hung low, hands cradling my face in a desperate attempt to grasp onto the fading memories. I strain to remember the details, but only fragmented flashes of what was happening dance through my mind like ghosts in the shadows.

In the dream, I am strapped to a cold, metal gurney, surrounded by blindingly bright lights that sear through my vision. A harsh, relentless buzzer blares in the background, echoing through the empty corridors of my subconscious. I shake my head vigorously, as if I can banish the unsettling images from my consciousness by sheer force of will.

Glancing at the clock, its illuminated numbers mocking me with their reminder of the unearthly hour, I realize it is three in the morning. The darkness outside presses against the windows, a silent witness to my inner turmoil. A heavy feeling settles in the pit of my stomach, a premonition whispering that today will be different, that today will not be a good day.

With a sigh, I rise from the bed, the room's chill sending shivers through my entire body. With a stretch and a wide yawn, I make my way to the bathroom. I feel the cool tiles beneath my bare feet. I turn the shower on, letting the steam fill the cramped space, a feeble attempt to cleanse myself of the lingering unease that clings to me like a second skin.

As the scalding water cascades over me, I close my eyes, hoping to wash away the remnants of the dream that still haunts my mind like cobwebs in the dark corners of a forgotten room. But try as I might, the memory slips through my grasp like water through clenched fists, leaving me with an unshakable sense of foreboding.

Today will indeed be a day like no other, a day where the line between dreams and reality blurs, and the shadows that haunt the fringes of my mind come creeping into the light. But I will face it head-on, armed with nothing but the fragments of a dream and the unwavering resolve to uncover the truth that lies hidden within the recesses of my restless mind.

Eight Days Earlier

I head to the coffee shop early, feeling the cool morning breeze on my face as I approach the familiar spot. It's not an incredibly special place, but it holds a special spot in my heart for the familiar faces and friends I've made here over the years. As I push open the door, the rich aroma of freshly brewed coffee envelops me, instantly putting me in a better mood. Chaz, the barista, greets me with a warm smile as I approach the counter.

"The usual, my friend?" he asks, already knowing the answer.

I chuckle, comforted by the routine.

"Sure, uh, do I have a usual?" I inquire, pretending to be surprised.

Chaz laughs,

"Well, of course you do. You have ordered the same thing every day for the past 365 days. Today qualifies you as having a usual. Coffee black with a small yogurt."

I smile sheepishly, realizing I am indeed that predictable.

"I guess I am," I admit. "So, what's new with you? Did you enjoy your vacation a few weeks ago?"

Chaz starts preparing my order. He nods, his eyes lighting up as he recalls his time off.

"I did, laid-back and uneventful, just like I like it. It was good to recharge and unwind."

As we are engrossed in conversation, a breaking news alert suddenly blares from the TV above the counter, catching everyone's attention. The reporter's urgent voice fills the cozy coffee shop, announcing,

"We interrupt this program with breaking news." The screen flickers to life, showing footage of a major event unfolding in the unfamiliar city.

Chaz muttered under his breath, "Well, there's one less dictator to worry about."

Chaz and I exchange curious glances, our coffee forgotten momentarily as we listen intently to the developing news. The reporter's words ring with a sense of urgency and concern:

"The leader of a Middle Eastern country was killed in a massive earthquake."

As the gravity of the situation sinks in, the once-bustling coffee shop falls into a hushed silence, the only sound being the reporter's voice echoing through the room. As we watched the news coverage together, united in a moment of shared concern, I stood frozen, the coffee cup halfway to my lips, processing Chaz's comment. My eyes darted around, searching for any reaction from the other patrons. Chaz, unfazed, calmly walked away to assist another customer, leaving me to ponder his words.

The reporter's voice droned on, "... largest earthquake in their history ..."

I couldn't shake Chaz's nonchalant response. Was he joking, or did he know something more?

The front of the shop is lined with windows so patrons can sit, drink coffee, and watch folks walk to and from their destinations. In a state of dissolution, I turn and find myself a cozy spot by the door and sipping on my black coffee. Sitting at my window seat, the bright morning sun feels harsh against my unsettled thoughts. Chaz's words echoed in my mind, raising questions I never thought I'd have to consider over a cup of coffee. As I ponder the last few minutes that transpired, all the regulars begin to descend on our small gathering place.

As they enter the door and pass by me, I speak as I would with every patron as they arrive. The first one through the door is Fred Shirman. "Hi Fred, how’s the pet business going?"

"Good. Most people's bark is worse than their bite," Fred chuckles, his eyes twinkling with humor. He has a three-year-old boy and is full of Dad jokes.

I begin to pull my thoughts back into a more realistic mindset. I nod, glancing over to where Jennifer is engaged in an animated conversation with a group of young adults.

"Hi Jennifer, still hitting home runs on social media?"

"It's not easy helping people who think they can soar like Eagles but can only waddle like ducks." She is the type who pulls no punches; she says what she thinks before she thinks it through.

As I sit and stare out the large plate window, my mind continues to drift to the conversation I had with Chaz earlier. He made a mysterious comment predicting what a reporter would say about a rogue leader in a Middle Eastern country. How did he know? He is a retired geologist and worked as a military contractor. I heard the old guys reference him once as Nightwatch. That definitely aroused my curiosity and deserves research. I make a mental note to ponder on this later and add it to the collection of mysterious tidbits I've gathered over the months.

I have always had a knack for observing people. I find joy in soaking up snippets of conversations, deciphering body language, and guessing occupations or life stories. It's like piecing together a puzzle of human behavior, each interaction adding a new piece to the puzzle. The morning sun streams through the windows, casting a warm glow over the bustling street outside. People of all shapes and sizes pass by, each with their own story to tell. I take a deep breath, feeling grateful for the simple pleasure of being a silent spectator in this vibrant complexity of life.

As the day progresses and patrons leave for their various jobs around town, the coffee shop empties out. Carol Humsetler, the self-proclaimed world-traveler, bids farewell to Brooks, leaving with a mysterious air about her. With curiosity getting the best of me, I decided to do some sleuthing of my own. I asked Chaz, the barista, about Carol's habits. "What do you know about Carol? What does she do for a living? Where is she from? With each question, he avoided answering. Just a little smile and murmurs,

"I'm not sure."

Then, after pressuring him further, he still holds back.

"The only thing I know is that she always receives a small piece of paper from a different person in the coffee shop each morning." I could tell he was agitated.

"Okay, you are holding up progress. That's enough questions."

With that, he returned to the counter and continued serving coffee and pastries to patrons.

As I sit in my window booth with my computer, I dig deeper into Mrs. Humsetler's past. I uncovered a few unsettling things from articles in the Observer News archives.

It seems she was arrested at a protest against a private firm she once worked for. The article says she was released without prejudice, but she no longer worked for the firm. Years later, another article states she was involved in a distortion or cover-up at the State Department. How does one go from working for a private company to working for the State Department? Intrigued, I consciously tell myself to pay closer attention to Carol tomorrow. As I left the coffee shop, I couldn't shake off the feeling that there was more to Carol's stories than met the eye.

Seven Days Earlier

The next morning, I arrived at the coffee shop earlier than usual, eager to observe Carol's interactions. Like clockwork, she entered right on time. She greeted the usual friends as she does each day. Finally, what I was waiting for: Today, she shook hands with Brian and received the familiar piece of paper. This time, I managed to catch a glimpse of the seal and a word on the paper before she crumpled it and stashed it away. I approached Carol during a lull in her conversation and offered a casual chat. We talked about travel, her favorite destinations, and her experiences. When I mentioned the note she received, she seemed momentarily taken aback but quickly composed herself.

Before I could ask any probing questions, she excused herself and left abruptly. It was clear that I had stumbled upon something more significant than idle chatter about travels. Determined to get to the bottom of this mystery, I delved deeper into my investigation. I spent hours researching Arabic connections to the word "iitlaqnar" and its possible implications in Carol's context.

The puzzle pieces slowly began to come together, revealing a hidden world of intrigue and danger I had never imagined in my quiet coffee shop. As the hours passed by, I continued to eavesdrop on conversations and piece together snippets of information. Each new detail added a layer of complexity to the unfolding mystery surrounding Carol and her enigmatic morning routine.

Six Days Earlier

The next morning could not come quickly enough. As I arrived at the coffee shop, Carol walked in behind me. She walked straight over to Fred. She tried but couldn't hide that she had received the usual note, and, as I prepared to leave, I mustered the courage to confront her. I walked up to her and asked about the significance of the notes." She looked around at the other patrons to see who was watching us.

"I don't know what you are talking about."

"Each morning you greet people, and each morning one of them gives you a note."

"You mean this?" She handed me the note. "It's our birthday list I'm organizing, and this month it's Chaz."

Sure enough, it said Chaz, December 3, 1959. With doubt in my voice, "This isn't what I saw the other day. Yesterday I noticed the word iitlaqnar on the note."

Then, to my surprise, Carol's demeanor changed, and she pulled me over to a secluded booth in the corner.

"I know you have been snooping around in my past. You do not want to get involved with this, so I suggest you back off and forget everything. This is bigger than you can or want to take on."

She reluctantly revealed that she was a retired airline stewardess who used her cover as a world traveler to gather valuable information for a covert operation. The notes she received contained coded messages that directed her next moves in the high-stakes game of espionage she was entangled in.

As Carol bid me a hasty goodbye and disappeared into the bustling streets, I was left stunned by the realization that my seemingly mundane surroundings harbored such thrilling secrets. From that moment on, I couldn't help but wonder what other hidden dramas played out beneath the surface of everyday life, just waiting to be uncovered by a keen ear and a curious mind.

Five Days Earlier

The morning sun cast a golden glow through the coffee shop windows, highlighting the faces of four older gentlemen gathered at the high-top tables near the east wall. They were a formidable group, unmistakably retired service men by the jackets and hats they proudly wore. Major Gower, a Marine with insignia gleaming, met my gaze as I observed them from afar. I offered a lazy salute, to which he responded with a firm,

"Semper Fi."

Intrigued, I delved into the meaning of the Marine Corps motto, learning that it signified

"Always Faithful."

Armed with this knowledge, I planned to reply with a hearty "Oorah" whenever the Major greeted me.

Among them was Lieutenant Bannier of the Air Force, identified by the bars on his jacket collar. Under his breath, he murmured to one of the others about my presence, deeming me

"A little creepy."

Two of them are survivors of the battleship Arizona. Now, Captains Moler and Harman bear the scars of Pearl Harbor, their valor immortalized through their stories.

And there is the General, sporting two shiny stars on his cap, a silent testament to his distinguished service. I overhear their reminiscences of battles fought and sacrifices made, transporting me to bygone eras of heroism and patriotism. The men, bound by a brotherhood forged in the fires of war, shared anecdotes of valor and camaraderie.

Four Days Earlier

The next morning, they beckoned me to their table, inviting me into their world of valiant escapades and covert missions. As they regaled me with tales of daring encounters and secret operations, I was in awe of their courage and resilience. They painted vivid pictures of a past filled with danger and intrigue, their voices alive with the echo of battles long fought. Despite their advanced years, there was an unmistakable aura of vitality that surrounded them, as if they could still be called to action at any moment.

Their stories transcended time, blurring the lines between past and present, immersing me in a world of heroism and sacrifice. As I listened to their tales, I realized that these men were not just legends of the past; they were living heroes whose valor continued to inspire all who knew them. And so, I sat among them, humbled by their presence, grateful for the opportunity to glimpse the true essence of courage and loyalty that defined their lives.

If I didn't know better, some of the stories they tell could very well be of battles fought in the past weeks, not from decades ago, stored in their minds to recall while reminiscing about a past life.

One of the men, a grizzled warrior with scars etched deep into his weathered face, spoke of a time when he stood alone against an overwhelming enemy force. His eyes sparkled with raw emotion as he recounted the desperate struggle, his voice cracking with the weight of the memory. I could hardly believe that this man, now sitting calmly sipping coffee at a small shop in this nondescript town, had once faced such unimaginable danger.

Another man, his hands calloused from years of maintenance on a battleship, shared a story of sacrifice and brotherhood that brought tears to my eyes. He spoke of a time when he had risked everything to save his fellow soldiers, knowing full well the likely outcome of his actions. The depth of his bond with his fellow warriors was evident in every word he spoke, a bond forged in the crucible of battle and strengthened by unwavering loyalty.

As the morning wore on and the sun's rays through the windows moved across the floor, more stories were shared. Tales of daring escapes, last-minute rescues, and impossible odds overcome filled the air.

Forging a legacy of valor that enveloped us all.

Each man bore the marks of his past struggles, whether physical or emotional, and yet they sat together as living testaments to the enduring power of the human spirit. As I sat among these living legends, I realized that their stories were not just tales of battles won and enemies vanquished. They were stories of resilience in the face of adversity, of sacrifice for the greater good, of love and friendship that goes far beyond even the deepest divides. These men were more than just warriors; they were embodiments of everything good and noble in the world.

In that moment, surrounded by such greatness, I felt a profound sense of gratitude wash over me. To have been granted the privilege of hearing these stories, of witnessing the strength and courage of these men firsthand, was an honor beyond measure. And though I knew that their tales would someday come to an end. I also knew that the legacy of their heroism would live on, inspiring generations to come.

And so, as our time drew to a close and the sun began to fade into darkness, I sat in silent awe of these living heroes. Their spirits burned bright in the darkness, lighting a path for all who dared to follow in their footsteps. And as I bade them farewell and watched them disappear into the night, I knew that I would always carry their stories with me, a reminder of the boundless potential within each of us.

Three Days Earlier

The next morning, when I arrived, I was greeted by the brothers Jay and Brian, who are the epitome of successful siblings, running their family's accounting firm with precision and dedication. Despite their similar academic backgrounds and professional pursuits, their personalities couldn't be more different. While Brian thrived in the world of business and numbers, Jay is the life of the party, always in search of the next adventure.

I have tried for years to get their firm to sponsor a show at the theatre. They never took me up on the offer. Several times, I invited them to shows to get to know them better and to acquaint them with the benefits of partnering with our firm in the community.

On this particular Thursday evening, the routine at the accounting firm was broken when Jay unexpectedly accepted tickets to a theatre show I had offered. Of course, this sparked curiosity among the staff. The whispers spread like wildfire as he arrived with a stunning woman on his arm. It was clear that Jay was not one to turn down a good time, but his presence at the theatre that night seemed more than just a casual outing.

After the show, I invited him for a drink at the bar, and to everyone's surprise, he agreed. As the drinks flowed and inhibitions lowered, Jay began to share cryptic stories with me. Though his speech was slurred, I could understand him very well.

“You know, a mysterious underground network is operating right under everyone's noses.”

His words were laced with danger and urgency, leaving me both fascinated and unnerved.

In a rare moment of vulnerability, and in a drunken slur,

“You know, I had a recent near-death experience.”

He was alluding to some sort of force that could have led to his death. As I pressed for more information, Jay's demeanor shifted, a flicker of fear in his eyes. Realizing he may have said too much.

“You have got to forget this conversation and carry on as if nothing was revealed.”

What Jay doesn’t know about me is that as I gather information, I don’t forget it, I can’t forget it. It stays with me like files on a computer.

Two Days Earlier

The next day was a bright, bustling morning at the local coffee shop, filled with the usual sounds of clinking cups and voices mingling. As I entered, my gaze swept across the room, noting familiar faces scattered throughout the space. I ordered my usual coffee and yogurt, but I couldn't shake the lingering unease from the previous night's encounter.

The mysterious network Jay had alluded to weighed heavily on my mind, sparking a curiosity that could not easily be dismissed. As minutes turned into hours, the memory of that peculiar evening with Jay lingered, prompting me to delve deeper into the secrets veiled beneath the surface of the two brothers' seemingly ordinary lives. What began as an innocent encounter at a theatre evolved into a mysterious journey of discovery, leading to unexpected revelations and unsettling truths that would forever alter the course of our intertwined destinies.

Chaz was deftly preparing orders behind the counter, the group of retired gentlemen was engaged in their daily banter, and Jennifer and Fred occupied their regular spot at the high-top tables. Oddly, Jay was missing from the scene, which left me uneasy. Irrational thoughts flitted through my mind as I tentatively approached the counter, where Chaz waited to take my order. As I requested only black coffee, a departure from my routine, Chaz's eyebrows raised in surprise.

"Really? Coffee black? No yogurt today?" he inquired, his curiosity was overwhelming.

The weight of everyone's eyes on me felt palpable as I noticed their subtle glances in my direction. With my coffee in hand, I settled into a seat by the window, but the warmth of the cup of coffee could not compete with the chill that crept up my spine. A wave of paranoia washed over me as I thought about the connection of this seemingly ordinary group of individuals. Could there be more to them than I could comprehend? Were they concealing a clandestine world beneath their mundane lives?

Ridiculing my own thoughts, I chuckled softly, dismissing the notion of a group of seemingly disparate locals being entwined in some grand conspiracy. Yet, as I observed the eclectic mix of patrons and their behaviors, a nagging sense of curiosity lingered. Sipping my coffee, I let my imagination wander, envisioning wild scenarios of espionage and intrigue involving the elderly regulars, the bickering young couple, the meticulous accountants, and even the affable barista. The idea seemed preposterous, yet the notion refused to be entirely extinguished.

As the morning progressed, the lively chatter of the coffee shop enveloped me, drowning out the whispers of doubt that lingered in my mind. Perhaps it was merely a figment of my imagination, a concoction born of an overactive imagination seeking excitement in the ordinary.

Nevertheless, as I savored the last drops of my black coffee, a seed of curiosity was planted, leaving me to wonder if there was more to this small town and its inhabitants than met the eye.

My mind was reeling from the information I had gathered, but I was surprisingly not overwhelmed. Later that evening, I visited a clandestine website and purchased a listening device. A small in-ear unit that picks up on radio waves and transmissions from devices that are meant to be hidden from the general public.

The Day Before

When I arrived at the coffee shop, I ordered my usual. I stood there dumbfounded as Chaz eyed the earpiece I was wearing suspiciously. He quickly whirls around the counter and grabs my arm.

"What is that in your ear?"

I hastily mumble,

"It's just an earbud for listening to music."

I try to pull away, but his grip on my arm tightened. Chaz's expression tells me he knows there's more to it. He leans in closer, his voice barely a whisper,

"Do you know what can happen if you delve too deeply into things you shouldn't?"

His words send a shiver down my spine, and I feel a knot form in my stomach. What had I stumbled upon? Was the peaceful face of this little town hiding something sinister beneath the surface?

I collect my things and make a hasty exit; the consequences of Chaz's warning weigh heavily on my mind. As I sped away in my car, my thoughts were a whirlwind of questions. What was the secret behind that unassuming coffee shop? Why did the mere presence of that listening device set off such a chain reaction? The puzzle pieces refuse to align, leaving me with a creeping sense of unease.

I can't shake the image of the patrons staring at me, their gazes following me even as I vanish into the distance. It's as if the whole town is cloaked in a veil of mystery, a tangled web of secrets waiting to be unraveled. I realize then that my curiosity may have led me down a dangerous path, that I may not be able to turn back from. But the burning need to uncover the truth propels me forward, my heart pounding with a mixture of fear and exhilaration.

As the road stretches out before me, I steel myself for the journey ahead, knowing that the answers I seek may lead me into the very heart of the unknown. I know they gather daily, at the same time and place, but does that mean anything? So many questions and no answers. A light pops on in my head. Wade, Wade will know what to do. I head straight to see Wade. He has probably been through this before. When I arrive at Wade's house, he is on his knees, busy working in his flower garden. He loves clipping flowers and trimming shrubs. I jumped out of my car and ran up his sidewalk. I grabbed his arm, almost out of breath. He stands up calmly, with a half smile.

"I knew you would come to see me sooner rather than later, but it's not me you are looking for."

He hands me a plain white card with nothing on it. I look at it with a blank stare.

"What is this?"

He replies.

"Hold it in the sunlight."

As I hold it in disbelief, writing appears after a few seconds.

"It's an address, go to that address for the answers you are looking for."

He takes me by the shoulders, turns me around, and gives me a little push. I make my way back to my car. Sitting in the cool of my car, I stare at the paper, which is blank. The address looked familiar. I held it out the window in the sunlight, and the address reappeared. I've seen this address before. I put it in my GPS and headed there with apprehension.

As I make the last turn, it comes to me: this is Brooks' address. I slowly pulled into his driveway. As I cautiously ascended the steps to the grand front door of the imposing mansion, I couldn't shake the feeling of unease settling in the pit of my stomach. Before I could even raise my hand to knock, the door swung open slowly, revealing a tall, mysterious figure silhouetted against the warm light streaming from inside. It's Brooks.

"I've been waiting for you to arrive," he spoke softly, his voice carrying a stern yet welcoming tone. "Come inside."

Without hesitation, I stepped across the threshold, my eyes adjusting to the excessiveness of the lavishly decorated den. Intricately designed tapestries hung on the walls, exuding a sense of history and mystery. Brooks motioned for me to follow as we navigated through the den and into a long hallway that seemed to stretch on endlessly. Eventually, we arrived at a door tucked away under a winding stairway.

With a bit of uncertainty, he swung the door open and gestured for me to enter. As I did, my shirt caught on a small nail protruding from the door frame, causing a sharp scratch on my upper arm. Ignoring the pain, I followed him down a dimly lit staircase that descended two flights below the ground.

What lay before me took my breath away. A sprawling room filled with row upon row of computer screens, more than I had ever seen in one place. The screens cast an eerie glow over the entire space, resembling the command center of a top-secret government agency.

"Is this real? Is this really real?" I whispered to myself, still unable to fully comprehend the surreal scene before me. Monitors lined the left wall, displaying complex data streams and security feeds from around the world. It was a control room straight out of a spy movie, yet it was undeniably authentic.

He broke the silence as I tried to make sense of the situation.

"Welcome to my domain," he said, his eyes reflecting a mix of pride and determination.

"I have been watching, waiting for someone like you to join me in this endeavor."

On each computer screen, a different person,

"Hey, that's the coffee shop. THAT IS CHAZ. There are the tables at the coffee shop."

One monitor has an overview of the entrance, and another is trained on the back entrance.

"Brooks, what is going on? Why do you have all this in place? Why are you monitoring these people? Most of all, why are you showing me all of this?"

"Well", he starts, "this thing has grown bigger than one person can handle, more than one person can control. Until now, I have collected intel and used sources to control information in and out, and I have had good success. Now they are getting stronger and smarter, and the danger is growing and spreading much more than one person can control."

The more I ask, the more he explains, and the deeper I get into something I'm not sure I want to be part of. An hour passes as we look into the lives of these unsuspecting patrons of this nondescript coffee shop. He interrupts my curious inspection of the control room to ask me a question. Not the question I expected. He didn't ask if I wanted to be part of the solution, or if I wanted to help in some way, or what I thought of all of this. He asked a simple three-word question:

"Can you breathe?"

I unconsciously and instantly take a deep breath. I answer defiantly,

"Yes."

As I anxiously look around the room, my chest becomes tight, my breathing becomes shallow, and I look at Brooks.

"What is going on?"

I go to one knee and grab my chest. Brooks leans down and injects me in the neck with a small device. Almost immediately, my breathing eases, and I stand up. I take a swing at him and miss as he backs away. I grab my bicep,

"That was not an accidental scratch when I entered the staircase, was it?"

"No, it was a lethal dose of Hyetholchloridesuplex 9, a drug that constricts the tracheal tube and causes death within minutes when activated. The shot I just gave you is the first antidote and lasts 24 hours. Talk to anyone about anything you have seen here, and there will be no second dose. Choose to ignore the situation totally, and you will breathe your last breath in exactly twenty-four hours from ten minutes ago."

"Twenty-four hours, that's not enough time. I

need to figure this out."

"Twenty-four hours, choose not to join us, and we will attempt to wipe your memory and reverse the effects. Sometimes it works, and sometimes it doesn't. You really do not want the latter of the two possibilities. I'm sorry, but I don't know of any other way. This is how I was recruited as well. You jumped into this, poked around, and discovered more than we were comfortable with. When you had discovered enough to bring you to me, that is far too close. The Hyetholchloridesuplex 9 is the assurance that you will be loyal to the Crew. I think once you learn what we are about, you will totally understand."

He hands me a card.

"Call this number tomorrow. If you decide to be on the side of covert justice, all will be good. Not all things are as they seem, you know."

As I leave, I look at my watch and set the timer for twenty-three hours and thirty minutes. I have just twenty-three hours to find out all I can about a guy I know almost nothing about. Where do I start? What do I know as facts? I know he is independently wealthy. I know he has been retired for years. Because he mentioned traveling to his different houses around the world for the last few years, he has two daughters; his wife was the CEO of a large conglomerate. As time passes, I look through hundreds of pages of notes I have taken over the past months and thousands of pictures I have taken, cataloged, and filed.

The Day Of

With weary eyes and no sleep, time is getting close. I look at my watch, 6:05 am. With no other leads, I head to the Coffee Shop, hoping to hear something I haven't heard before. Maybe someone will react or say something to help me understand this crazy mess I've gotten into. As I enter, I head straight to the counter. Chaz greets me.

"The usual, coffee, black, and yogurt?"

"Uh, just coffee, black."

I turn and quickly sit in a booth close to the door. As the regulars enter, I watch every eye, every facial expression, every turn of the head, and everybody's gestures. It seems everyone has arrived just as they have over the last few days. Nothing seems to be out of the ordinary, nothing out of character. Everything is as normal as it has been for months. This seems wrong; this is too normal. As I decide to leave and give in to the fact that I am no closer now than I was, I look at my watch and almost blurt out,

"Only thirteen minutes left."

I have just thirteen minutes to get to Brooks'. If this is true, I now only have twelve minutes to breathe my last breath. I race out the door. As I do, I grab my phone from my back pocket, and I hurriedly dial the number on the card he gave me twenty-four hours earlier. I almost dropped my phone. I fumbled with it in my hands as the ringing stopped, before he could answer.

" I am on my way, I am within ten minutes."

The ten-minute drive seems like an eternity. I keep looking at my watch as the timer counts down. It seems as if everything is in slow motion, as the numbers on the timer click off faster and faster.

I arrived at his driveway, and I glanced at my watch. I have three minutes to spare. I open the car door, jump out, and stumble over the curb. I hurriedly walk up three steps to his front door. Again, I look at my watch, two minutes and twenty-nine seconds. I ring the doorbell and glance at my watch once again, two minutes and eight seconds. I ring the doorbell again and knock at the same time.

I turn my watch to look at the face, one minute thirty-nine seconds. Why isn't he answering? Did I wait too long or push it too close this time? I start breathing deeply, and I feel my heart beating faster. I look at the timer, fifty-six seconds left. I beat on the door with the side of my fist and rang the bell continuously. I take several deep, quick breaths, knowing they will be my last. Time slows as I look at my watch. It clicks to 00.00... I slowly fall to my knees as everything fades into darkness.

I feel as though I'm floating on a cloud. I can feel motion, but I can't move. It's as if I'm held down with restraints; I struggle to move, but can't. Is this death? Have I died, and am I on my way to my final destination, my final resting place?

The darkness is blinding; there is nothing but darkness. I yell out, but nothing comes out of my mouth. What is happening? Why can't I move? Why can't I speak or see? Is this eternity?

It seems like a second is an hour, an hour is a day. No sense of time or space. Slowly, my eyes adjust to the darkness, and I wake to blurry vision and a powerful headache.

Without warning, the lights come on, blindingly bright white and flashing. A piercing, high-pitched buzzer is blaring in time with the flashing light. I try to sit up, but I am restrained. As I struggle with the straps holding me down, I feel motion. We are moving in some sort of vehicle; instinctively, I know we are moving south. Since regaining consciousness, we have traveled 1.2

miles. That calculates out to 126 MPH. The flashing light stops along with the buzzer. The door to the right of the stretcher opens. It's Brooks, and behind him is Wade. They both enter the room with a look of anxiety and optimistic hope, all while the transport continues. I strain to raise my arms and sit up with all my strength. The straps win the battle as I forcefully ask,

"What is happening? Why am I tied down, and where are we headed?"

They both stand there with no expression on their face. I note that Wade's heart rate has accelerated, and his breathing has hastened. Finally, Wade breaks the silence and replies.

"Can you breathe?"

This time, unlike the last, I can breathe, no shortness of breath, no racing heart.

"Yes, I can breathe, now untie me and let me up."

"We had to test you, we had to know if you are who we need you to be. Without a test, there is no advancement, promotion, or increase in skill and knowledge."

Brooks unties me, and I sit up slowly.

"The headache will subside, and blurry vision will clear in an hour or two. Just take it easy for a minute while we brief you on the situation. But first, are you in or are you out?"

As I sit on the edge of the table with my face in my

hands, I have to think. I have struggled with this all night, asking myself what it all means. Good vs evil, right vs wrong. For some reason, I know they are on the right side of justice; they are on the side of good. I'm not sure if they go by the book on everything, but I do know they are on the right side of what I believe in. Knowing I don't have much choice at this point, I raise my head and answer,

"I'm in."

Brooks starts with,

"Very soon, the knowledge you have gained and the information you have gathered will make more sense. Some of the things we are going to tell you may seem strange."

Wade begins with what seems to be a story from a science fiction movie.

"After years of rigorous research and testing, the scientists of our organization have finally discovered a way to enhance human abilities through the use of specialized enzymes. These enzymes can only amplify the innate skills that a person already possesses, pushing them to their maximum potential. The problem is that it also amplifies both good and evil. After numerous trials on different individuals, they stumbled upon someone exceptional, someone who showed extraordinary proficiency levels in every skill test, and also a positive mental attitude to work for good."

Brooks interjects, “The chosen individual is you.”

“Me, why me?”

“Listen to us, then you can ask questions.”

“You were given a small injection of these ground-breaking enzymes. You immediately experienced a surge in your learning capabilities. Within minutes, your mind absorbed information at an unprecedented rate, delving into realms of knowledge previously unimaginable.”

Brooks walks to the left side of the gurney.

“For example, you have been calculating the speed and distance we are and have traveled. You have and are analyzing your surroundings with unparalleled precision, and it is already becoming second nature to you. Every detail in the room was recorded in your memory with flawless accuracy, from the instruments on the walls to the subtle fluctuations in our personal vital signs.”

Wade hands me a bottle of water and begins.

"Under the careful guidance of the crew, you will hone your newfound abilities with astonishing speed. In a matter of days, you will be deemed ready to take on the most crucial role within the organization - heading the enigmatic division known as T.H.E.A.T.R.E. You had been strategically placed in this position a decade ago, under the guise of merely being a director of a local theatre.”

Confusion clouds my mind as they inform me of my true purpose.

"How can I be the director of an organization I know nothing about?"

"As we have explained, the theatre was merely a front, a cover for our real operations. Through hidden surveillance in a local coffee shop, we have been observing not only you individually but several others, all being groomed for the same destiny, to be crew members of T.H.E.A.T.R.E. Tactical Headquarters for Encounters of All Temporal Resonance on Earth."

Wade adds, "Sound is a powerful tool and can also be a powerful weapon."

As the realization dawned upon me, a mix of astonishment and apprehension settled in. The prospect of becoming the Director of T.H.E.A.T.R.E seemed daunting yct exhilarating. With my enhanced abilities and the organization's unwavering support, I stand on the precipice of a profound journey, ready to unravel the mysteries and challenges that await in the shadows of these extraordinary capabilities.

Day One:

September 14th, 2009. On my first day as the Director of T.H.E.A.T.R.E., I arrive at work, just behind me, Caroline and Dave, my lighting and audio engineers. Betty, my trusted assistant, pushes past us, arms full and with the nervous energy of three people her size.

"Out of the way, out of the way. These people are not going to wait all day."

She hurriedly opens the office for business as she has each morning for the past year. People are lined up outside the box office window, hoping to get the first and best seats available for tonight's show. Betty settles in, boots the ticketing computers, and begins selling tickets to the anxious, crowded line that has gathered in the early morning.

This is one of the biggest concerts we have produced since the opening of the "THEATRE". We are all in show mode, as we are each day hosting a concert, but today will be a little different. The concert will be underway in just nine hours. Everyone is busy doing what it takes to present a national artist to a sold-out concert hall.

Though producing a live concert of this caliber is stressful, the concert itself is no different from the hundreds we have done before. The twist with this concert is that we discovered just twenty-four hours ago that this concert will be broadcast worldwide to fifty-six countries and simulcast on over one thousand domestic and foreign radio stations.

Along with such large-scale productions, an array of problems can arise that seem to multiply by the hour. Issues that can genuinely be unbelievable. From dealing with the opening act and coddling to the headlining artist's daily needs and wants.

Orchestrating a sound check for a sometimes pretentious individual can more than double the pressure. The phone rang again, interrupting the hectic pace set for the day.

Betty almost yells over my headset,

"It's for you, line four, and it's marked urgent."

With apprehension, I pick up the phone, and the voice on the other end says only three words:

"The Fourth Wall."

This, a theatre term, is an imaginary wall separating the actors from the spectators, but not in this case, not on this line. This line is reserved, reserved only for the crew of T.H.E.A.T.R.E. These three words are code meant for the new Director.

The voice on the phone is one I recognize well; it is Brooks, the head of T.H.E.A.T.R.E. With these three words, I know several things. We are on the verge of an attack or have been attacked. Our crew has been called upon to engage the unknown, to attempt to stop a threat from the deep underworld. And we are the first line of defence.

As a member of T.H.E.A.T.R.E., an agency dedicated to upholding the highest of standards set forth by an agency of truth, light, and honor, we are asked to take the lead in solving or diverting a disaster. As this is my first time at the helm, T.H.E.A.T.R.E. is needed and will gladly serve to ensure a safe transition and coherence of resonance in our world.

I place the phone back in its cradle and head backstage. As I walk, things change. I feel as if I'm in slow motion; I open the door that leads into the theatre, the lights dim, and the colors change almost to sepia or a reddish hue.

Everything is so detailed; I start gathering information as I walk. I glance over to the Front of House position, and Delay is in place at the sound board, getting ready for the show. I notice the position of each fader, each meter setting, every cable plugged in, and every setting on the crossover. I realize his heart rate is slightly high at ninety-five per minute and rising. His breathing is up to twenty-four breaths per minute. Is he having trouble?

Four steps more, and again I glance to the right, this time to the lighting position, DMX is there, and programming her console for the show tonight. I see she has 46 scenes programmed, her heart rate is 63 per minute, and her breathing is normal at 14 per minute. She is calm and steady as she is during every show. Little does she know she will soon be under assault along with Delay and the rest of the crew, as we are one team, one unit. Our team works best together, under fire as one, especially when a crisis arises.

I walk through a set of black drapes and then down a spiral staircase; I reach the entrance to our control center, and a plain black panel with green lights appears to the right of the door. I place my right hand on the panel; it scans my palm, then I enter a special code, which opens the door to the hidden secure bunker.

The control room for the Tactical Headquarters for Encounters of All Temporal Resonance on Earth. I enter the pitch-black room, and I can't see a thing except for a tiny green flashing light near the doorway. Almost instinctively, without thought, my reflexes took over; I extended my hand to touch the light. As soon as my fingertip made contact, a soft hum reverberated in the room, and suddenly, the once dark space began to illuminate.

To my astonishment, rows of computers, wide-screen monitors, and a centralized main console came to life. The mesmerizing glow filled the room as I made my way to the central seat in front of four computer monitors. With a swift, focused motion, I contacted each remote office of T.H.E.A.T.R.E. individually, the screens flickering with data.

As I navigated through the system, tapping away on the keyboard, a feeling of exhilaration coursed through my veins. Among the chaos of flashing lights and buzzing screens, I found myself immersed in a world of technology and information, like a conductor orchestrating a symphony of connectivity.

In that moment, within the glow of the digital realm, I felt empowered, as if each keystroke held the key to unlocking endless possibilities. The once-dark, mysterious room had transformed into a realm of endless capabilities, waiting to be used.

As I sit at the control board, I start gathering information. I sent a simple text to each head of the extended branches.

"We Have A Mission."

Each member of T.H.E.A.T.R.E checks in,

"DMX, here up and running."

"Delay here, ready to make some noise." Stagehands respond,

"Locked, loaded, and ready."

Abruptly, on the fourth monitor, it's Bannier, our contact at B.P.R.D. (Bureau of Paranormal Research and Defense.) He is under attack and visibly distressed; he gasps for his last few breaths. He describes what sounds like the end of our existence as we know it.

"We are being invaded by a force unknown to any database we have access to here at the Bureau."

He struggles to speak. "Nothing… has affected it… in any way, nothing has… destroyed it; nothing has even phased it at all."

Struggling for air and with what seems to be his last breath: Bannier OUT.

More monitors show disturbing scenes from other departments.

Four hours ago, we were told a test of the emergency broadcast system would be sent out over all electronic devices around the planet at 2 pm Eastern Standard Time. Without warning, the test was sent out three minutes early at 1:57 pm. It all began at B.P.R.D., marking the start of the attack.

This time, I think we have our work cut out for us. We were hit from all sides. It came from everywhere, and no warning or alarms sounded at all. They have taken out the main coupling to the matrix at B.P.R.D.

I pull up Delay on the headset. "We will need to reroute all transmissions and video through a new patch if you can find one."

"Looking Now"

I respond, almost yelling through the com system. "We are still under attack, and our agents are falling fast. If you cannot stop whatever is causing this attack quickly, we will lose every driver and diaphragm in the place."

I press a button labeled global channel announce.

"OK, guys, someone or something is trying to stop the largest gathering of world leaders seen in this millennium. No obvious clues have been left, and there is not much evidence at any of the scenes.

It's going to take all the resources of T.H.E.A.T.R.E. to solve this one. So what do we have so far?

Delay chimes in, "It all started with a break-in at Bureau Thirteen. Not a normal break-in, this was different. Nothing was taken, but something was left. Maybe just residual traces, but something was left. It shows up on the in-house oscilloscope recorders."

"DMX here, I checked the video from first thing this morning. As Moler arrived, he sat at his desk. The phone rang, he answered it, and two seconds later, he was history. No damage to the office, no files were destroyed or taken, only his life was taken."

"I just got a report from Harman at JBL (Justice Bureau of London), Gower was killed while on an annual hunting trip he takes with his family. Delay chimes in: "Also, within hours, two ambassadors from Sennheiser

Corp., a husband and wife team, Jennifer and Fred, were killed in a plane crash en route from Zurich, where they attended a meeting with Nightwatch."

"Now, the Department Head of B.P.R.D. is in critical condition at Bethesda. In less than four hours, we have lost four very influential and dedicated officials and one who doesn't have much of a chance to make it through the night."

DMX interrupts:

"What do these people have in common? Is it a random act of violence to incite paranoia?"

Delay keys his mic;

"Maybe an act of terrorism from another agency or faction trying to take over, to maybe influence this world in a direction more in line with their own."

A low rumble starts around 80 hertz. I jump into the chatter,

"Or can it be a plot from within our own agency to realign the structure and direction we are headed? This has been attempted several times in history; the latest was in the early 1960s with the assassination of President John Kennedy. The plot fell apart before it got far enough along to fully develop and was blamed on a lone gunman."

Delay interrupts, "We all know that was not the case, remember the grassy knoll? We have chosen, for various reasons, not to pursue the evidence and simply accept what we are told, For Now."

My thought is,

"The familiar pattern of single one-off strikes has altered. This time, it is different. This time, there are multiple attacks and multiple deaths, leaving us all scrambling to make sense of the carnage."

DMX keys in,

"The masterminds behind these meticulously orchestrated assaults have opted for a new strategy."

Without pause, I add, "Yes, one that bewilders even the most seasoned crew. Instead of targeting the usual high-profile figures or institutions, they are disrupting the chain of command on many fronts at once."

Delay chimes in,

"No place is safe from their calculated wrath."

As the crew grapples with the unprecedented wave of assaults, a sense of fear and uncertainty tries to overcome us all.

The distortion has grown to 400 hertz and 83 db.

Who could be next? Who will be next? Where will the next strike occur? These questions haunt the crew's collective consciousness, casting a shadow of doubt over a once-confident, able group.

We have been assembled to unravel the enigma behind these synchronized attacks. Each member brings a unique set of skills to the table, all driven by a shared determination to bring the perpetrators to justice.

What seems like hours of tireless pursuit, T.H.E.A.T.R.E. begins to piece together a complex web of connections, leading them closer to the elusive culprits.

Clues emerge from the most unlikely of places, cryptic messages hinting at the motives behind the chaos that is gripping the situation in a deadly embrace.

As the tension mounts and the stakes grow higher, the distortion grows as well, now at 800 hertz and 94 db. It becomes a race against time, pitting the forces of law and order against a shadowy enemy whose reach seems to know no bounds. The fate of the show hangs in the balance, teetering on the brink of either salvation or utter devastation.

In a final, heart-stopping showdown, T.H.E.A.T.R.E. confronts the masterminds behind the terror that has a stranglehold on us in its iron grip. A battle of wits and wills unfolds, culminating in a moment of truth that will determine the future of all involved.

Outside forces know our organization has many heads. We can survive any single loss, but maybe by breaking the chain in many links, somehow, chaos will ensue. Is Bannier the last, or is the list much longer? Who will be next?

"DMX, maybe you can shed some light on the situation. Pull all video and lighting records for each of the attacks."

"I'll also cross-reference the times and location of each, with special care given to the order in which they were hit. Maybe that will give us a clue as to the next in line."

"Delay, start working on all audio transmissions in and out of each office." (Delay has a funny look on his face, but before he says anything, I say, "Yes, including the ones we have planted as well."

A big smile comes on his face as Delay replies,

"Just checking. I will also check out the remaining four Heads of State before, during, and after the attacks to see if anything peaks the meters."

"Both of you send a couple of stagehands to check out their homes and families. Also, check on any contact they have had with each other in the past six months. If the last six hours are any indication of the next six, we will run out of time fast."

The distortion is now at 1.5 hertz and 101 db. It has become very uncomfortable. We almost need to yell over the intercom to be heard.

"DMX, please tell me you have configured the lights and routed everything for maximum visuals on our video system."

"Yes, sir, I have, and I also have access to three of the four key computers and cameras in the House and Green Room. Ah, the fourth is coming online now."

"Delay, we have audio?"

"Working on it, one, two, three, yep, all four are up and running."

Information starts coming in at an unbelievable rate.

Delay reports:

“We have a hit, no two, three, four. We have hits coming in from all over the place.

“This can't be actual data I'm seeing. If so, hundreds of cells have developed in just a few hours. Both of you, run a level three, no wait, a level 5 diagnostic on all subroutines. If this is accurate data, we ourselves will be hit in just a few seconds.”

Delay has to yell to be heard over the disturbance: “All subroutines running at optimum.”

DMX does the same:

“Here, as well, everything seems to be optimized.”

Just as suddenly as it started, it stopped. (Almost at the same time and with a puzzled look on their faces, both Delay & DMX say,

"They're gone," everything is clear.”

“What the hell's going on? First, they're here, then they're gone.”

Delay keys in,

“No hold on, they are returning, this time with vengeance. This time, even stronger, 112 dB at 16 kHz, we are going to lose it if something doesn't give. The sound is deafening; it is so loud that we have to yell through our headsets just to be heard. We can barely make out what the other is saying.

“Delay, try dropping the gain a few Db and try to isolate this crap. We must have a clear signal for more than a few seconds to get through this, or we are fighting a losing battle. Go back and cross-reference the audio just before Moler was killed with audio on the plane that crashed on its way back from Zurich."

DMX asks, "What are you looking for, boss?"

"I'm not sure, but Delay will know when he hears it." (Humans can hear sounds ranging from roughly 20 Hz to about 20 kHz. Delay can hear between 1 Hz and 140 kHz.)

Delay with his head tilted to one side slightly,

"Hold on, I think I have something. A few seconds before the phone disconnects, there is some sort of interference. This could have been achieved with a high-frequency resonator device with a controlled tone, set high enough that it could be configured to kill."

DMX, "Also a witness on the hunting trip with Harman, describes what sounded like a gunshot followed by a high-level sound wave burst. By the time the other hunters got to him, he was dead."

Delay interrupts, "I have seen this once before. When sound waves from two different sources meet, they can reinforce one another where the peaks coincide and cancel one another out where the peaks meet the troughs, creating an interference pattern with loud and quiet areas. If the vibrations have different frequencies, this can create a pulsed effect or a "beat" in the combined sound."

I interrupt Delay. "Don't give me the whole book right now; just break it down. What exactly do you have?"

"Well, that is what is heard in the few seconds just before the phone disconnects."

"OK, so what does that mean?"

"After cross-referencing that sound with our master database here at T.H.E.A.T.R.E, I have a match. The only other time we encountered this was when we came up against that rogue agent who defected a few months ago, Carol Humstler. We have given her the nickname DISTORTION!"

"DMX, do we have anything on the plane crash?"

"Evidently, something interfered with the harmonics of both engines to the point of collapsing the airstream intake. This brought them down like the Hindenburg."

"Do you think rogue agent Distortion is behind this attack as well?"

"I'm not sure, but it sure seems so."

"Delay, pull all cables from each send, patch them through a different route, and see if that helps."

"DMX, if your systems are functioning properly, pull up the last few encounters with Distortion and see if it affected the normal routines running at that time."

DMX yells back: "Already done. If I recall, we had to replace every multiplex and duplex controller we had in place. She really wreaked havoc all around the world that week."

"Delay, any progress on your end? Time is running close."

Delay keys his mic, "I think I have it now. I have traced her to an abandoned peripheral unit that we no longer use but is still in the chain. I'm pulling all connections to and from that unit. This should squash her like a bug in the corner."

Delay with a look of relief on his face says, "DMX, Go to the main board, on the channel strips, press the select buttons in this order: 1, 9, 16, 4, 23, 11, and 5. I have replaced several of the main circuits and rerouted the aux sends through the T lines to the main crossover. This will eliminate about 90 percent of the interference; the rest I can filter out with the outboard equalization unit in the main rack. If all these checks out, the authorities should be arriving at Distortion's location in less than a minute to take her into custody."

The ear-piercing, high-pitched loop suddenly stops. A bright flash of light, then my eyes slowly adjust to normal. I'm standing on stage with a microphone in my hand. The sepia effect is gone, and everything looks and feels, for lack of a better term, normal. Dave is at FOH along with Caroline at the lighting board.

Dave's voice comes through the monitors. "Hey, Boss, you OK? You looked like you were in another world there for a minute."

"I couldn't move for a sec. Yeah, yeah, I'm

good...CHECK, CHECK, Hey, Hey, Check 1,2,3 Check. I think we have our feedback distortion problem under control now. Can somebody grab the band from the dressing room and tell them it's time for sound check? We have a show to do in less than 60 minutes. Let's roll, people. We don't have time to lollygag!!!!"

I think to myself, once again, T.H.E.A.T.R.E has prevailed, repelled another attack, and another crisis has been averted. For now, we are somewhat safe. We have lost some good men, but we will live to fight another day. As the dust settles and the echoes of chaos fade into the distance, we may emerge forever changed, hopefully for the better. It's a scary reminder of the harrowing ordeal we have endured. But through the darkness, a glimmer of hope shines bright, a testament to the resilience of those among us who refuse to surrender to fear.

Music plays in the background as I walk off stage and head to my perspective spot for tonight's show. As I pass the front-of-house position, I glance over to the main console. The faders move on their own, and the words "FOR NOW" appear on the console screen.

At 3 a.m., I wake in a cold sweat, my heart racing, and I struggle to make sense of the jumbled images flashing through my mind. I sit up abruptly, the remnants of the haunting dream still lingering in the air around me, elusive and disorienting. It is the same recurring dream that has been plaguing me for weeks, a puzzle without a solution.

I find myself sitting on the edge of the bed, my head hung low, hands cradling my face in a desperate attempt to grasp onto the fading memories. I strain to remember the details, but only fragmented flashes of what was happening dance through my mind like ghosts in the shadows.

In the dream, I am strapped to a cold, metal gurncy, surrounded by blindingly bright lights that sear through my vision. A harsh, relentless buzzer blares in the background, echoing through the empty corridors of my subconscious. I shake my head vigorously, as if I can banish the unsettling images from my consciousness by sheer force of will.

Glancing at the clock, its illuminated numbers mocking me with their reminder of the unearthly hour, I realize it is three in the morning. The darkness outside presses against the windows, a silent witness to my inner turmoil. A heavy feeling settles in the pit of my stomach, a premonition whispering that today will be different, that today will not be a good day.

With a sigh, I rise from the bed, the room's chill sending shivers through my entire body. With a stretch and a wide yawn, I make my way to the bathroom. I feel the cool tiles beneath my bare feet. I turn the shower on, letting the steam fill the cramped space, a feeble attempt to cleanse myself of the lingering unease that clings to me like a second skin.

As the scalding water cascades over me, I close my eyes, hoping to wash away the remnants of the dream that still haunts my mind like cobwebs in the dark corners of a forgotten room. But try as I might, the memory slips through my grasp like water through clenched fists, leaving me with an unshakable sense of foreboding.

Today will indeed be a day like no other, a day where the line between dreams and reality blurs, and the shadows that haunt the fringes of my mind come creeping into the light. But I will face it head-on, armed with nothing but the fragments of a dream and the unwavering resolve to uncover the truth that lies hidden within the recesses of my restless mind....

About the Author

As an artisan, I honed my pottery and woodworking skills independently, finding solace and fulfillment in creative pursuits during my leisure hours. My distinguished career as a journeyman tool and die maker provided a solid foundation, complemented by four decades immersed in the vibrant world of entertainment promotion. Capping this journey, I have served for the past fifteen years as the Executive Director of a thriving Art Deco theatre, originally built in 1939, where I book and present musical performances for large and enthusiastic audiences. Long days and nights were spent working, drinking coffee, and living the dream, and this book is a result of some of those long nights.

Acknowledgments

My deepest gratitude goes to my wife, family, and friends, whose unwavering faith in me, a novice writer, sustained me through countless late nights and endless revisions.

Ironically, a significant turning point came from a high school journalism class. My classmates suggested I abandon the journalism and writing course and pursue other avenues after high school. It's a testament to the power of perseverance that, after 47 years, I've finally returned to this passion. This journey proves that the dreams of youth, however dormant, can blossom at any age.

Finally, and most profoundly, I owe an immeasurable debt to my mother, whose boundless belief in my potential and her consistent encouragement to embrace new challenges. Her unwavering belief in my capabilities instilled in me the courage to pursue my ambitions. Her words, "You can accomplish anything," echoed through the years, propelling me forward and fueling this improbable journey.

Thanks for reading! Please add a short review on Amazon
And let me know what you thought!

Other books by Stan Lowery: "Lady In White: The Final Curtain Call" and
"A Theatre's Plea: From Dereliction to a Dream"
Find them on Amazon

Let's have coffee!

www.ingramcontent.com/pod-product-compliance
Lightning Source LLC
LaVergne TN
LVHW010841120826
845149LV00020B/3442

* 9 7 9 8 9 9 4 6 0 9 2 0 0 *